Lloug Sibbitt

Jerome

BY PHILIP RESSNER

ILLUSTRATED BY JEROME SNYDER

PARENTS' MAGAZINE PRESS • NEW YORK

BY THE SAME AUTHOR

August Explains

Dudley Pippin

At Night

for my mother

One day in a pond in a summery green hollow, a big frog named Jerome was sitting catching flies when a witch came by.

"Hello, old witch," Jerome said.

The witch didn't like to be called a witch. She looked at Jerome with silvery eyes and smiled a mean smile. "It's not nice to call people witches," she said.

"Well, I'm sorry," Jerome said.

"I could turn you into something awful for saying that," the witch said. "But I think I'll turn you into a prince instead."

"Well, I don't mind," Jerome said.

"We'll see," said the witch, laughing to herself. "We'll see." And she waved her crooked black stick in the air and began to sing a strange tune without words. Soon a great wind sprang up and the pond began to bubble slowly like hot oatmeal. Then it all stopped and Jerome was still a frog.

"Am I a prince now?" he asked.

"Of course you are," said the witch.

"But I don't feel like a prince," Jerome said.

"Oh, you will," said the witch, laughing up her flappy sleeve. "You will. Now, you just go on into town and see what happens."

So Jerome did as the witch said, and when he came to town he said, "Hello, I'm the new prince who does princely deeds."

The townspeople laughed to themselves because they saw that he was just a frog. But they said to Jerome, "So you're a prince who does princely deeds? How would you like to do some for us?"

"At your service," Jerome said.

"Good," the people said. "Now, the first thing we want you to do is get rid of a terrible giant crow who eats up all our corn before we can harvest it." Then they took Jerome to a field where the corn swayed light green and fragrant in the sun, and they left him to wait for the crow.

Soon an enormous crow landed nearby and immediately began to eat the corn.

"Stop," Jerome shouted. "Stop eating the corn."

The crow looked over his shoulder, still munching. Then, after a bit he swallowed and said, "I never talk with my mouth full; it's bad manners."

"It's bad manners," Jerome said, "to eat corn that doesn't belong to you."

"Well, I know," said the crow. "But I'm very large for my size and it takes a lot to fill me up. Also," said the crow, leaning down near Jerome's ear and whispering, "I'm very worried that everybody else is going to eat up all the corn before I do. How about you, for example; wouldn't you like to get your teeth into all this nice juicy corn?"

"Not me," Jerome said. "I'd rather eat flies."

"Honest to goodness?" said the crow.

"That's right," said Jerome. "And I promise never ever to eat any corn. How about that?"

"Why, that's just fine," said the crow.

"I also know some fish who will never eat corn," Jerome said. "And at least eight beavers, a couple of dozen foxes, and a whole tribe of frogs. And I know for a fact that all lions, tigers and whales would be happy never to eat corn."

"Hooray!" shouted the crow. And then he flew off in a great flutter of wings, whistling tunes he remembered from a long time before, when he hadn't worried about every-body eating up his corn.

After that, Jerome went back to the townspeople and told them that the crow wouldn't be eating all their corn anymore, but just some of it every now and then.

And the townspeople said, "That's fine; now how would you like to do another princely deed?"

"At your service," Jerome said.

"Good," the people said. "There is a greasy dragon who breathes fire and smells terrible. We would like you to slay him because he burns up our houses and forests."

"All right," Jerome said, and the people gave him a sword and took him to a dark cave in the side of a black mountain. "The dragon lives in there," they said, and then they ran to hide behind some rocks further off.

Jerome stood at the entrance of the cave and called in, "Dragon, come out at once! I am going to slay you."

After a while the dragon poked his head out of the cave and blew just a little puff of pink flame with smoke to match. "Why?" he said.

"Because," Jerome said, coughing a little from the smoke, "you have been burning the people's houses and forests."

"Well," the dragon said. "It's my nature." He poked Jerome with a greasy green paw. "You know what I mean?" he said. "I just can't help burning things, no matter how hard I try."

Jerome nodded and thought for a while. Finally he said, "Why not burn *other* things?"

"What else is there to burn?" the dragon asked, shaking himself impatiently and giving off a swampy smell.

Jerome stepped back a little. "Well," he said. "How about burning garbage at the town garbage dump?"

"Hmm, garbage," the dragon said, half to himself. "Does it smell deliciously awful?"

"Yes," Jerome said. "And there are piles and piles of it outside of town. Great heaps of it."

"Does it burn easily?" asked the dragon.

"Well, no, it takes some doing to get it started," Jerome said. "It's sort of damp."

"Good," said the dragon. "I like a challenge; lead me to it."

So Jerome led the dragon to the garbage dump, where the dragon puttered about poking at the garbage and peering and sniffing into things and pretending that he hadn't yet made up his mind.

But he already had, and he soon settled down happily to the job of burning the town garbage, which he did every Tuesday and Thursday, resting and telling lies on the other days of the week.

After Jerome had stopped the dragon from burning houses, some of the people began to say that maybe Jerome really was a prince. "Maybe," they said, "he really is a prince."

But most of the people still laughed. "Faugh, he's just a frog."

In spite of this they asked Jerome to do one more princely deed. It was a cold day, and the windows chattered in their frames, and the people said to Jerome, "We want you to do something about the wicked wizard who lives in the dark wood and does terrible things. You take the path to the left where it branches."

So Jerome took the path to the left
and soon came to a stone tower
that had no door and no win -
dows. At the top, looking
over the edge, was the

wizard. He had yellow eyes and mean ears. "Who are you?" he asked in a mean voice.

"I'm the prince who does princely deeds," Jerome said.

The wizard said to himself, "Ha, he's a frog. I can smell a frog when I see one." Then he said to Jerome, "What were you before you were a prince?"

"A frog," Jerome said. "What were *you* before you were a wizard?"

The wizard put on a large pair of green spectacles and peered down at Jerome. "Well," he said after a long time, "I guess I was a boy."

"Oh," Jerome said. "Why did you stop?"

"Well, being a wizard seemed as if it might be fun," the wizard said. "But it's not."

"That's too bad," Jerome said. "I'm sorry. Was it fun being a boy?"

"Oh," said the wizard. "Was it ever! Sunshine and thunderstorms; blue skies and green skies; secret codes and watermelon and horse chestnuts; telling stories under the porch; old aunts who smelled like flowers; summer mornings before the world was awake; and running downhill so fast you couldn't stop. Oh, I wish I were a boy again!"

The wizard had forgotten that when he wished for things they really happened. There was a thunder of lightning, the dark wood turned pale lavender, and the wizard turned into a boy with red hair. "I," shouted the boy, "am going to run downhill so fast I can't stop." And in a moment he was gone.

When the townspeople heard that Jerome had performed his third princely deed and that the wizard was gone, they decided that he must really be a prince, even though one who looked like a frog.

"Hooray for Jerome the prince," they shouted, and they gave him a little castle made of green stone with an even greener vine climbing on it.

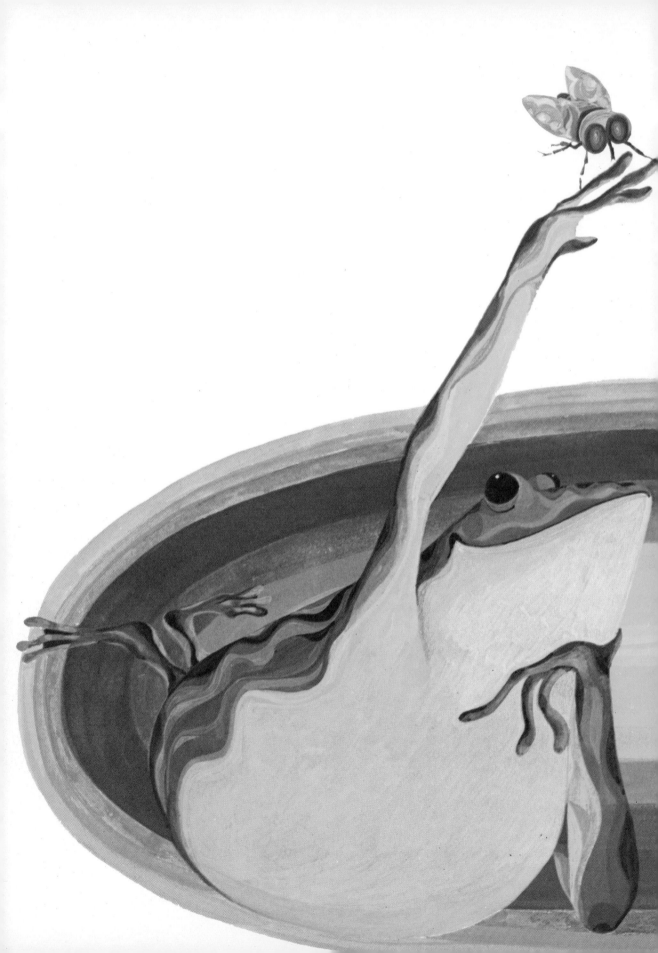

Jerome lived happily in it for a long time, and he particularly liked the pond in the backyard that was green and summery and full of flies.